Bear on a Bike
Oso en bicicleta

Stella Blackstone
Debbie Harter

Barefoot Books
step inside a story

Bear on a bike,
As happy as can be,
Where are you going, Bear?
Please wait for me!

Oso en bicicleta,
está muy feliz,
¿Adónde vas, Oso?
¡Por favor espérame!

I'm going to the market,
Where fruit and flowers are sold,
Where people buy fresh oranges
And pots of marigold.

Voy al mercado,
donde venden frutas y flores,
donde la gente compra naranjas frescas
y macetas de caléndulas.

Bear on a raft,
As happy as can be,
Where are you going, Bear?
Please wait for me!

Oso en una balsa,
está muy feliz,
¿Adónde vas, Oso?
¡Por favor espérame!

I'm going to the forest,
Where fearsome creatures prowl,
Where raccoons play and bobcats snarl
And hungry foxes howl.

Voy al bosque,
donde temibles criaturas merodean,
donde los mapaches juegan, los linces gruñen
y los hambrientos zorros aúllan.

Bear on a wagon,
As happy as can be,
Where are you going, Bear?
Please wait for me!

Oso en una carreta,
está muy feliz,
¿Adónde vas, Oso?
¡Por favor espérame!

I'm going to the prairie,
Where wild buffaloes roam,
Where graceful eagles soar and glide
And prairie dogs make their home.

Voy a la pradera,
donde los búfalos salvajes vagan,
donde las elegantes águilas se elevan y planean
y los perritos de las praderas hacen su hogar.

Bear in a steam train,
As happy as can be,
Where are you going, Bear?
Please wait for me!

Oso en un tren de vapor,
está muy feliz,
¿Adónde vas, Oso?
¡Por favor espérame!

I'm going to the seaside,
Where children love to play,
Where young friends dig and race
And swim, while fishes dart away.

Voy a la costa,
donde a los niños les encanta jugar,
donde los amiguitos cavan, corren
y nadan, mientras los peces se alejan veloces.

Bear on a boat,
As happy as can be,
Where are you going, Bear?
Please wait for me!

Oso en un bote,
está muy feliz,
¿Adónde vas, Oso?
¡Por favor espérame!

I'm going to an island,
Where magic star fruits grow,
Where herons fish in secret groves
And sparkling rivers flow.

Voy a una isla,
donde crecen las mágicas carambolas,
donde las garzas pescan en bosquecillos secretos
y ríos destellantes fluyen.

Bear in a balloon,
As happy as can be,
Where are you going, Bear?
Please wait for me!

Oso en un globo,
está muy feliz,
¿Adónde vas, Oso?
¡Por favor espérame!

I'm going to a rainbow,
Where the earth meets the sky,
Where the clouds turn into rain
And bright-winged parrots fly.

Voy a un arco iris,
donde la Tierra se encuentra con el cielo,
donde las nubes se convierten en lluvia
y los loros de alas coloridas vuelan.

Bear in a carriage,
As happy as can be,
Where are you going, Bear?
Please wait for me!

Oso en un carruaje,
está muy feliz,
¿Adónde vas, Oso?
¡Por favor espérame!

I'm going to a castle,
Where night is turned to day,
Where princes and princesses dance
And merry music plays.

Voy a un castillo,
donde la noche se convierte en día,
donde los príncipes y las princesas bailan
y la alegre música suena.

Bear on a rocket,
Flying through the night,
Wherever you are going, Bear,
Goodbye and goodnight!

Oso en un cohete,
vuela a través de la noche.
Adondequiera que vayas, Oso,
¡adiós y buenas noches!

Vocabulary / Vocabulario

bike – la bicicleta

raft – la balsa

wagon – la carreta

train – el tren

boat – el bote

balloon – el globo

carriage – el carruaje

rocket – el cohete

Barefoot Books
294 Banbury Road
Oxford, OX2 7ED

Barefoot Books
2067 Massachusetts Ave
Cambridge, MA 02140

Text copyright © 1998 by Stella Blackstone
Illustrations copyright © 1998 by Debbie Harter
The moral rights of Stella Blackstone and Debbie Harter have been asserted

First published in Great Britain by Barefoot Books, Ltd
and in the United States of America by Barefoot Books, Inc in 1998
The bilingual Spanish edition first published 2014
All rights reserved

Graphic design by Jennie Hoare, Bradford on Avon, UK
and Louise Millar, London, UK
Reproduction by B & P International, Hong Kong
Printed in China on 100% acid-free paper
This book was typeset in Futura and Slappy
The illustrations were prepared in paint, pen and ink, and crayon

ISBN 978-1-78285-079-3
British Cataloguing-in-Publication Data:
a catalogue record for this book is available from the British Library
Library of Congress Cataloging-in-Publication Data
is available under LCCN 2013030330

Translated by María Pérez

1 3 5 7 9 8 6 4 2